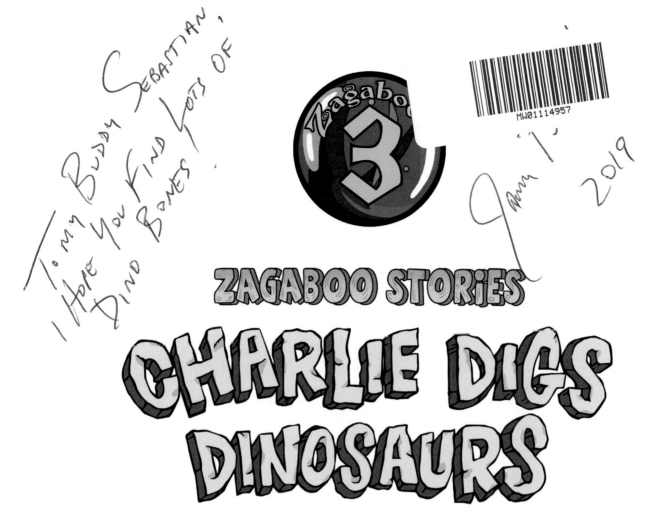

ZAGABOO STORIES

CHARLIE DIGS DINOSAURS

This book is dedicated to all the children who love to dig in the dirt. Adventure and discovery await you!

Order a junior-sized *Dirty Digging Hat* to go with this book!

Visit Zagaboo.com
For more books, toys, and music!

Charlie loved dinosaurs. He often went to the museum where he could see the fossil skeletons of Stegosaurus, Brachiosaurus, and Triceratops. His favorite dinosaur, though, was Tyrannosaurus rex, which he called T. rex. T. rex had the biggest sharpest teeth!

Charlie would sometimes meet paleontologists at the museum. Paleontologists are the people who find and dig up dinosaur fossils. Charlie dreamed of one day becoming a paleontologist and digging up a T. rex skeleton, just like the one in the museum.

Charlie's Uncle Doug was a paleontologist. When Uncle Doug heard how much Charlie loved dinosaurs, he invited him to his dig site. Charlie was really excited, but he was also a little nervous. He had never dug up dinosaur fossils before and didn't know how to do it.

The night before his visit, Charlie talked with Uncle Doug on the phone. "What if I mess up? What if I break a bone or something?" he asked Uncle Doug.

"Don't you worry, kiddo, you're going to do great!" Uncle Doug assured him. "But if you want to prepare for tomorrow, you should visit Zagaboo and his trolls."

Charlie was confused. Did Uncle Doug just say something about trolls? What did trolls have to do with anything? "Umm, what are you talking about Uncle Doug?" Charlie asked.

"You've never heard of Zagaboo?" Uncle Doug responded with surprise. "He's a troll king, of course. He rules an underground kingdom of trolls who know how to do just about anything, including paleontology. I should know! I visited Zagaboo's Kingdom when I was your age. I received my first paleontology lesson from a troll there named Dr. Razz. He called me 'Wee Doug' because I was so small."

Charlie laughed at Uncle Doug's funny nickname.

"You can learn paleontology from Dr. Razz, too!" Uncle Doug continued. "I'm sure he's still there, since trolls don't age."

Charlie thought this all sounded a bit crazy. "Are you serious, Uncle Doug? I've never heard of underground trolls who teach paleontology."

"Absolutely!" said Uncle Doug, almost yelling into the phone. "You should see for yourself! When you go to bed tonight, tug your ear and say, 'Zagaboo, Zagaboo, where are you?' If you do that, Zagaboo will send Dr. Razz to bring you back to Zagaboo's Kingdom to learn paleontology."

Charlie was skeptical, but he finally agreed to try calling on Zagaboo. After all, what harm could it do?

Later that night, after his parents had tucked him into bed, Charlie reached up and pulled his ear.

"Zagaboo, Zagaboo, where are you?" he said.

He sat up quickly and looked around his bedroom, waiting for Dr. Razz to appear. However, nothing happened. He tried again, but still nothing. All he saw was his stuffed T. rex at the foot of his bed.

Disappointed, Charlie pulled up his covers and closed his eyes. "I knew Uncle Doug was just kidding," he whispered to himself. Then he fell asleep.

Charlie wasn't asleep for very long.

"Charlie my boy, wake up. We have some digging to do!" said a raspy old voice.

Charlie's eyes snapped open. Standing on his bed was a little creature with fuzzy gray sideburns, big ears, and a dirty brown hat. Could it be? Yes! It was a troll!

"Are you umm…you umm…" Charlie asked in a shaky voice.

"No, sir! Of course I am not Yumm Yumm!" answered the troll. "Yumm Yumm is the vegetable troll. I'm Dr. Erasmus, the paleontology troll! But you can call me Dr. Razz. Are you ready to go to Zagaboo's Kingdom?"

Charlie stared blankly at the little troll, too stunned to say anything. He finally managed to nod his head.

"There's a good boy," said Dr. Razz.

Dr. Razz marched forward and tugged Charlie's earlobe. Charlie began to glow green, and then WHOOSH! He shrank to the size of a troll.

Charlie immediately kicked off his blankets and stood up on his bed. He looked around his room with amazement. Most of his toys were bigger than he was. His stuffed T. rex almost seemed real!

"Help me down off the bed, will you?" said Dr. Razz. "I'm not a young troll anymore, you know!"

"But I heard trolls don't age," said Charlie.

Dr. Razz turned toward the boy. "You mean I've always been wrinkly and bald?" he asked with surprise.

"I think so," Charlie responded.

Dr. Razz looked up sadly at his hairless head. "Zagaboo made me look too old! Just because I dig up old fossils doesn't mean I should look like one!"

Charlie laughed at the crotchety old troll.

Charlie and Dr. Razz crept out of the bedroom, down the hallway, and into the living room. Dr. Razz crawled under the couch. Charlie followed.

Charlie jumped with fright when he saw a dirty rodent with bent whiskers and only one eye under there!

"Ahh!" he yelped. "What's that?"

"Oh, that's just 20/20. He's my pet gopher. He's going to bring us to Zagaboo's Kingdom through these tunnels," said Dr. Razz, pointing to a hole in the floor.

They climbed onto 20/20.

"He's super-fast, so hold on tight!" said Dr. Razz.

20/20 stomped his feet and zoomed down the hole at lightning speed.

The gopher zipped through the tunnels, turning left, then right, then right again.

Charlie felt like he was on a roller coaster, but this was way more fun.

Dr. Razz stopped 20/20 after a little while and got off to look around. Charlie followed. Dr. Razz didn't recognize these tunnels.

"You silly old gopher, you got us lost again!" complained Dr. Razz.

20/20 wasn't listening. He had wandered off in search of a juicy worm to eat.

"20/20 loves making right turns because he can only see through his right eye," Dr. Razz explained to Charlie. "Sometimes he makes too many right turns and gets everyone lost."

Charlie thought that was kind of funny.

Dr. Razz leaned over and listened to the ground with his big ear. "Hmmm, I can't hear Trollopolis. We must be very far away from Zagaboo's Kingdom."

Dr. Razz stood up, cleared his throat, and yelled into the tunnels. "Does anyone know where we can find Zagaboo's Kingdom?" His voice echoed up and down the corridors.

Soon, dozens of furry gray creatures scurried out of the darkness. Charlie noticed they had noses that looked like long pink fingers. Dr. Razz and one of the creatures whispered to each other.

Dr. Razz turned toward Charlie. "Charlie, these are star-nosed moles. They are going to show us the way to Zagaboo's Kingdom. However, they've never met a human before. They asked if they can take a look at you first. Is that okay?"

Charlie agreed. The star-nosed moles immediately pounced on Charlie and began feeling him with their fingery noses. It was like being tickled by a thousand hands. Charlie laughed and laughed until tears streamed down his face.

When the moles were done, Charlie stood up and brushed himself off. "Hey! You said they just wanted to *look* at me!" Charlie complained to Dr. Razz.

"Yes, that's definitely what I said," Dr. Razz responded with a giggle. "Charlie, my boy, star-nosed moles are blind. They see by feeling things with their special noses."

Charlie realized he'd been tricked by the little troll. At first Charlie was kind of mad, but then he started to laugh. After all, it was a funny trick. Plus, he thought the star-nosed moles were really cool.

Dr. Razz and Charlie climbed back onto 20/20. The star nosed-moles pointed to the left tunnel. 20/20 went left, reluctantly.

They eventually reached the entrance to a large cavern.

"We're here Charlie! We're inside Fossil Tunnel in Zagaboo's Kingdom!" Dr. Razz announced. "This is where we're going to do paleontology!"

Charlie climbed off 20/20 and looked around. His eyes widened. He saw dinosaur fossils sticking out of the walls, the ground, and even the ceiling!

"This is the most amazing place I've ever seen!" Charlie yelled out. Charlie pointed at the dinosaurs and began naming them. "There's Dreadnoughtus, with the long neck! And up there is Quetzalcoatlus, the biggest flying animal ever. Some people think it was a dinosaur, but actually it was a reptile! And there's Triceratops, with three horns. It used to have huge fights with T. rex!"

Charlie realized these fossils were all from the Late Cretaceous Period, 65 to 99 million years ago, when T. rex was alive. Charlie turned to Dr. Razz.

"Have you found a T. rex yet?" he asked excitedly.

"Not yet, my boy," Dr. Razz responded.

Charlie was bummed. He wanted to see a T. rex.

"Don't be disappointed," said Dr. Razz. "Right now I'm digging for a magical creature. No one has seen it for millions of years. I think I'm finally close to finding it."

A magical creature? That sounds fun! Charlie thought.

"It's a fish called Pappy Carp," Dr. Razz explained. "Pappy Carp lived in a lake with lots of shells. Using his hook fin, he would pick up shells from the muddy bottom and bring them to the surface for Shelltop Fairies to wear as hats. Shelltop Fairies are magical. They live in the huge tree above Zagaboo's Kingdom. The fairies told me that one day Pappy Carp left to collect a shell for the Shelltop Fairy Queen, but he never returned. No one knows what happened to him. Without Pappy Carp, the Shelltop Fairies had to find their own shells, which wasn't easy since fairies don't swim. They don't have to worry anymore, though. Our Swimming Trolls get their shells now."

Charlie really hoped they would find Pappy Carp.

Dr. Razz handed Charlie a bag of paleontology tools. "The hammers are to break the rocks around the fossils and the brushes are to clean off the bones," said Dr. Razz. "All you need now is a Dirty Digging Hat."

"A Dirty Digging Hat? What's that?" Charlie asked.

"It's a hat, of course!" Dr. Razz bellowed. "All paleontologists wear them!"

Dr. Razz opened his satchel and pulled out a brand new hat for Charlie. Charlie wondered why he called it a *Dirty* Digging Hat. It wasn't dirty at all.

As Charlie reached for his new hat, Dr. Razz dropped it on the ground. Then Dr. Razz stomped on it with his big troll foot. Stomp! Stomp! Stomp! When Dr. Razz had gotten the hat sufficiently dirty, he picked it up and placed it on Charlie's head.

"There you are, my boy. Your very own Dirty Digging Hat. Now you look like a real paleontologist!"

Charlie coughed as dust fell off his hat and onto his face.

Dr. Razz turned and began walking toward a different part of the tunnel. "Follow me!" he announced.

Charlie chased after him. They approached a large section of the tunnel wall where the rock was kind of pink and red.

"Different colored rock is called strata," said Dr. Razz, pointing at the wall. "Strata shows you where the fossils are. This pink and red part has lots of fish fossils in it, which means it used to be under water. I think this is where we'll find Pappy Carp. Let's start digging here."

Dr. Razz began breaking the rock with his hammer and sweeping away the broken pieces with his brush. Whenever he found a fossil, he would put it in his satchel. Charlie copied Dr. Razz.

Dr. Razz and Charlie found fossils of ancient catfish, frogs, and even a crocodile.

Charlie continued chipping away at the rock. Suddenly he saw a fossil he didn't recognize. It was big. Really big! He hammered around the fossil some more, and then brushed it off. It was a claw in the shape of a hook. *Could it be?* Charlie thought. *Is this Pappy Carp's hook fin?*

"Look, Dr. Razz. Look! Look!" Charlie called out. "I think I found Pappy Carp!"

Dr. Razz rushed over and examined the fossil. "You're right, Charlie! This *is* Pappy Carp!"

"Woohoo!" they both screamed, jumping into the air with excitement.

"What do we do now?" Charlie asked.

"We keep digging!" said Dr. Razz. "If we dig up the whole fossil, we might discover why Pappy Carp disappeared all those years ago!"

Charlie and Dr. Razz dug even faster than before. But it was still taking a really long time.

"This is a huge fossil!" gasped Dr. Razz. "We're going to need some help. Come here 20/20! Help us dig!"

20/20 grunted and turned up his nose. The gopher had no desire to work. He just wanted to relax and roll in the dirt.

"I'll give you a juicy earth worm if you help us dig up Pappy Carp!" said Dr. Razz, dangling a fat night crawler in front of the gopher.

20/20 darted over and quickly gobbled up the worm. The bribe worked! 20/20 was ready to help!

All three vigorously began digging. Rock chips flew into the air, zipping this way and that. Before long, the whole place had turned into a big dust cloud. When the air cleared, Charlie, Dr. Razz, and 20/20 stood back and looked at what they had uncovered.

"Look, Dr. Razz!" Charlie yelled. "Now we know what happened to Pappy Carp! He was trying to pull the shell off that big hermit crab, but the hermit crab wouldn't let go. They probably got stuck in the mud while fighting over the shell. They must have turned into fossils after that!"

"Charlie, my boy, I think you're right! I think that's what happened!" Dr. Razz said with a big troll grin.

Dr. Razz leaned over and whispered something to 20/20. The gopher stomped his feet and immediately sped off into the tunnels. Charlie wondered where he was going.

"I've been searching for Pappy Carp ever since a little boy named Doug came to Zagaboo's Kingdom many years ago," Dr. Razz explained to Charlie. "Doug thought Pappy Carp might be in this part of the tunnel because it used to be under water. I called the little boy 'Wee Doug' because he was so small." Dr. Razz chuckled to himself.

"Are you talking about Uncle Doug?" Charlie asked with excitement.

"Is Wee Doug your uncle?" asked Dr. Razz.

"Uh huh, he sure is!" Charlie screeched. "He's the one who told me to come to Zagaboo's Kingdom! He's not little any more, though! He's like, six feet tall or something! And he's a paleontologist!"

"Six feet tall and a paleontologist, you say?" asked Dr. Razz. "Well, that's great news! I had a feeling he would become a paleontologist! After all, I'm a great paleontology teacher! The extra growing magic I gave him seems to have worked, too!" Dr. Razz said proudly.

At that moment 20/20 returned to Fossil Tunnel. He was followed by a large group of Shelltop Fairies. The fairies talked excitedly about Pappy Carp as they gathered around Charlie and Dr. Razz.

Then all at once the fairies grew silent. A troll with orange clothes and a green beard emerged from the crowd. He walked toward Charlie.

Dr. Razz introduced Charlie to the troll. "Charlie, my boy, this is Zagaboo, king of the trolls!"

Charlie was awestruck. *Wow, King of the Trolls!* Charlie didn't know what to do, so he did the only thing he could think of. He took off his Dirty Digging Hat, got down on one knee, and in a shaky voice proclaimed, "Your majesty!"

Zagaboo and the fairies broke out in laughter. Charlie was confused. He wondered why they were laughing.

"You don't have to kneel to me, Charlie. I'm just Zagaboo!" Zagaboo stated.

Charlie blushed. As he got back to his feet, he noticed a tall fairy moving through the crowd. She had the largest, prettiest shell hat of all the fairies. She stood next to Zagaboo.

"Charlie," said Zagaboo, "it is my great honor to introduce you to Lanalla, Queen of the Shelltop Fairies!"

Charlie waved at the Shelltop Fairy Queen. "Hi, Lanalla!" he said.

The Shelltop Fairies gasped in horror.

"You're supposed to kneel and say *'Your majesty'* to the queen," Zagaboo whispered to Charlie.

Kneel, don't kneel. This was confusing, Charlie thought.

Queen Lanalla stepped forward. "Charlie," she said in a soft voice, "we have been searching for Pappy Carp for a very long time. Now, thanks to you and Dr. Razz, he is found."

Charlie and Dr. Razz smiled.

"Pappy Carp brought us our first shells," the queen continued. "That magnificent hermit crab shell was meant for me. But after millions of years, it has turned into a fossil. We shall leave it here with Pappy Carp, but we will return often to see it. You and Dr. Razz shall forever be heroes to the Shelltop Fairies."

"Congratulations, Charlie," said Zagaboo. "Not only did you find Pappy Carp, but you also learned why fossils are so important. They can tell us what happened long ago. I hope you find many of them throughout your life!"

Dr. Razz gave Charlie a big thumb's up.

"But right now we need to get you home," said Zagaboo. "You're scheduled to dig up dinosaur fossils with Uncle Doug in the morning."

Zagaboo lifted his marble staff, which started to glow, and placed it on Charlie's shoulder. "It is my pleasure," said Zagaboo, "to pronounce you Charlie, the great fossil finder and our newest Troll Paleontologist!"

The fairies erupted in cheer. They flew excitedly around the tunnel, swooping down and giving Charlie high fives. Charlie, Dr. Razz, and Zagaboo laughed and celebrated with the fairies. It was a great party!

But the festivities couldn't last forever. Zagaboo was right. Charlie needed to get home.

Charlie hugged Zagaboo goodbye. He then climbed onto 20/20 with Dr. Razz. Zagaboo and the fairies waved farewell as Charlie, Dr. Razz, and 20/20 raced out of Fossil Tunnel and back toward Charlie's house.

20/20 only got lost twice, so it didn't take long to get home. They came up under the couch in the living room. Charlie and Dr. Razz quietly tiptoed to Charlie's bedroom. They pulled themselves up onto his bed.

"Charlie, my boy, I'm going to need that Dirty Digging Hat back," said Dr. Razz.

"Really?" Charlie responded sadly. "I was hoping I'd get to keep it."

Charlie reluctantly took off his hat and gave it to Dr. Razz. Then he got into bed and pulled up his covers.

"I had a lot of fun digging up fossils with you," said Dr. Razz. "Don't forget to tell your friends to call on Zagaboo if they ever need help with anything!"

"I will," said Charlie.

"Now, close your eyes and think of your favorite dinosaurs," Dr. Razz told Charlie.

Charlie closed his eyes. The first dinosaur he thought of was T. rex, of course, then Triceratops and Brachiosaurus. Dr. Razz tugged Charlie's ear and Charlie slowly grew back to normal size. Charlie didn't realize it, but Dr. Razz had given him a little extra growing magic to make him tall, like Uncle Doug, when he got older.

When Charlie opened his eyes, it was daylight. He must have fallen asleep. Charlie sat up and shook his head, trying to remember what happened. He wondered if Zagaboo's Kingdom was a dream. He looked around the room and noticed something beside his bed. He leaned over and picked it up.

It was a hat! But it wasn't just any hat. It had a picture of Pappy Carp's hook fin on it! Dr. Razz must have given him a new Dirty Digging Hat! Charlie quickly burst out of bed, got dressed, and put on his new hat. He was eager to start doing paleontology.

Charlie gazed out of the car window as his mom drove him to Uncle Doug's dig site. He wondered if he was going to find some neat dinosaur fossils that day.

When they arrived, Uncle Doug came to greet Charlie. "Hey, kiddo! Welcome to the dig site!" he yelled out.

Uncle Doug introduced Charlie to the other paleontologists. They all smiled and waved. Charlie waved back.

"I see you brought your Dirty Digging Hat," Uncle Doug commented. "What's that on the front?"

"It's a picture of Pappy Carp's hook fin!" Charlie announced proudly.

Uncle Doug's eyes popped open. "You mean you and Dr. Razz found Pappy Carp?"

Charlie nodded.

"Woohoo! That's awesome!" Uncle Doug screamed, leaping into the air. "Dr. Razz has been searching for Pappy Carp since I was a little boy! Did you figure out why Pappy Carp disappeared?"

"We sure did," said Charlie. Charlie told Uncle Doug how Pappy Carp and the hermit crab got stuck in the mud while fighting over a shell. He also told Uncle Doug about the visit from Zagaboo and the Shelltop Fairy Queen, Lanalla.

"It sounds like you had great fun in Zagaboo's Kingdom," said Uncle Doug. "Well, we're going to have a lot of fun, too! Are you ready to dig up some dinosaur fossils?"

"You bet I am!" Charlie responded enthusiastically.

"Wait a minute, Charlie," said Uncle Doug. "There's a problem. You can't dig up dinosaurs with that hat. It's way too clean!"

Uncle Doug took off Charlie's hat and handed it to him. Charlie realized what he had to do. He threw his hat on the ground and stomped on it. Stomp! Stomp! Stomp!

Uncle Doug and the other paleontologists cheered. They took off their hats and stomped on them, too!

Uncle Doug then brought Charlie and the other paleontologists to a hillside where the rock had different colors.

"I know what those colors are, Uncle Doug!" Charlie yelled out. "Those are called strata! Fossils are in there!"

Charlie grabbed an extra bag of paleontology tools and eagerly started digging. The others joined in, hammering and brushing, hammering and brushing.

Fossils slowly began emerging from the rock. Most of them were small. But then Charlie saw a large sharp object. He looked closer. It was a tooth!

"Look everybody," Charlie yelled to the other paleontologists. "I found a tooth!" Charlie stepped aside so that Uncle Doug could examine it.

"You're right, Charlie," said Uncle Doug. "However, this is no ordinary tooth. This is from a T. rex! And it's the biggest T. rex tooth I've ever seen!" The other paleontologists burst into cheer.

"What do you think we should do now?" asked Uncle Doug, looking at Charlie.

"We should keep digging," said Charlie. "We need to learn more about the T. rex."

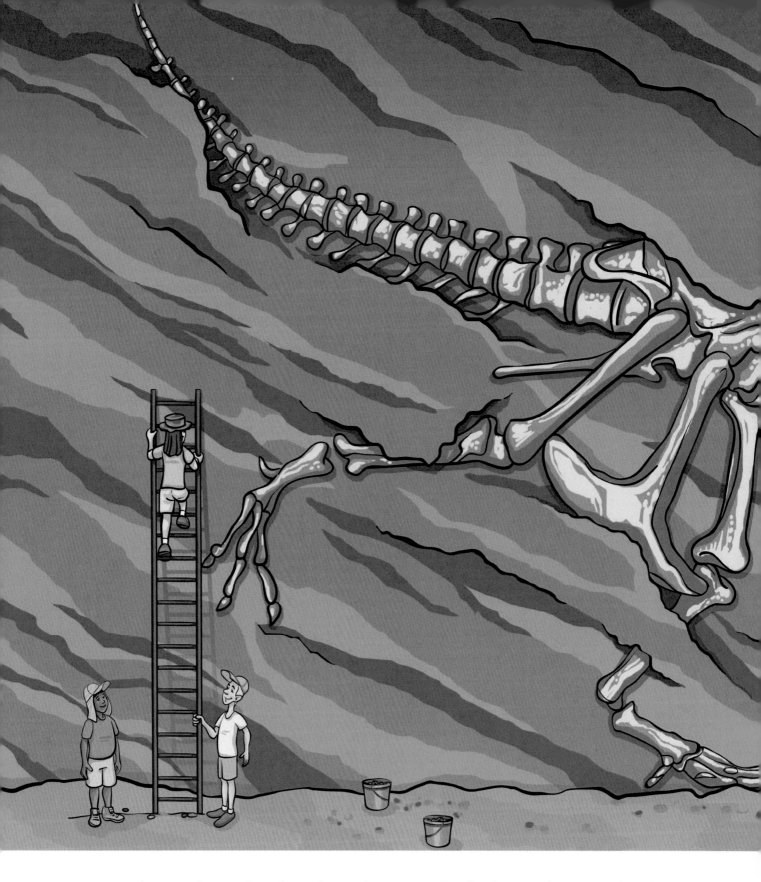

It took many hours, but the paleontology team finally dug up the entire fossil. That's when Charlie noticed a Triceratops horn stuck in the T. rex. "It looks like the T. rex got into a fight with a Triceratops and lost!" Charlie announced.

"That's right, Charlie," said Uncle Doug. "The Triceratops must have broken its horn off in the T. rex during the fight, and that's what killed the T. rex. This is an amazing discovery! It proves that even the biggest T. rexes weren't always the strongest dinosaurs. Everyone in the whole world is going to want to know about this!"

And Uncle Doug was right! News reporters from across the globe came to interview Charlie and Uncle Doug and take pictures of the T. rex fossil!

Dr. Razz and 20/20 watched everything from a nearby hilltop.

"Well, that proves it," Dr. Razz announced. "I'm definitely the greatest paleontology teacher in the world!"

20/20 grunted and rolled his good eye.

"I guess we should get back to Zagaboo's Kingdom now, just in case someone else needs our help," Dr. Razz told 20/20.

That sounded like a great idea to the gopher. After all, 20/20 was hungry and the tastiest worms could only be found in Zagaboo's Kingdom.

"Head for home, 20/20!" Dr. Razz called out.

The gopher stomped his feet, and dove head-first into the tunnel, turning immediately to the right.

Zagaboo's Kingdom was to the left.

THE END

94093368R00024

Made in the USA
Lexington, KY
23 July 2018